GW00976400

Dedication

This book is dedicated to my mother, who carried my family through difficult times. Thanks, Mom.

Acknowledgments

I'll keep this brief, in hopes that people may actually read it.

I'd like to thank Doreen Evans from Jemison Elementary for introducing me to some fine "children's literature" during story hour, Margo Gibson of Jemison High School for critiquing my earlier works, and Janis Cleckler (also of Jemison High School) for teaching me how to type so fast. Special thanks go to Helen Parish of Clanton's First United Methodist Church for helping me to appreciate God's creativity.

Also, I would like to especially thank Mike Zovath of Answers in Genesis, for his assistance in the publication of this book.

Oh, yes!

I would most of all like to sincerely thank Jesus Christ for the status of my salvation, without whom it would have been impossible.

The Lost World Adventures

BASED ON CHARACTERS BY
SIR ARTHUR CONAN DOYLE

ADAPTED & ILLUSTRATED BY
Mark Stephen Smith

Master
Books

First printing: January 2000

ISBN: 0-89051-277-9
Library of Congress Number: 99-67328

Printed in the United States of America

Please visit our website for other great titles:
www.masterbooks.net

For information regarding publicity for author interviews
contact Dianna Fletcher at (870) 438-5288,

Contents

Chapter 1

Dragonslayer

E xcept for the uneasy drizzle of the rain that trickled down the vines past Lord Roxton onto the riverbank, all was still. Lord George Roxton, a muscular gentleman in his mid-40s, tugged the brim of his hat down over his eyes to get a better look into the greyish gloom of the Amazonian rain forest ahead of him.

Anticipation, he thought.

He couldn't tell if this was the part of his job he loved most or hated least.

He wasn't acutely fond of reptiles, and even less so of the particular specimen he and his African companion, Zambo, were likely to encounter at any given moment.

The two men had come as missionaries to the native village mere miles beyond Manaus, the last outpost resembling civilization before the thicker, darker tangles of the jungle overtook the riverbanks. God's calling seemed to have drawn the two of them here, farther and farther up the river. The villagers to whom they had been assigned were preoccupied with an unwelcome visitor lately, and, as Zambo put it, a wolf seemed to be lurking among their flock. First, goats and cattle had gone — missing without a trace, and two weeks ago a fisherman was snatched from his boat, seemingly by some unseen force . . .

while four villagers watched in horror from the shore.

Lord Roxton had a suspicion it was a natural predator . . . not a supernatural predator, as the villagers seemed to believe. Being a Christian man, however, Lord Roxton was not so naive as to discount that the forces of spiritual warfare from time to time used physical agents . . . like reptiles.

Lord Roxton's experience wrestling crocodiles in his native Australia seemed to have prepared him for this moment . . . his unique service in the mission field.

The Scriptures that always caught his ears were usually those about serpents and dragons. They seemed to indicate that his destiny lay here in the jungle, and indeed, he believed in serving the natives through this current service, unusual and unexpected as it may have been.

"Here he comes," muttered Zambo, through gritted teeth.

"I see him," replied Roxton, grimly cocking his rifle. He leaned forward, ready.

Any less perceptive individual would have taken no notice of the slightly lazy stirrings of the river surface, and perhaps attributed them to troubled currents brought on by the rain.

However, as the underwater disturbance neared the muddy bank, the scaly coils of a serpentine back skimmed the surface, and near the head of the dark wake two dim circles seemingly gave forth a murky glow.

"He's a big one," Zambo commented, steadying himself for attack.

"Fifty feet?" inquired Lord Roxton, keeping his voice low.

"Sixty, or worse," replied Zambo.

At that moment, their bait, a wounded calf, suddenly seemed to take notice of the impending danger below the river's surface, and suddenly rose to give a frightened bleat.

With a swinging arc of foam, the head of a giant anaconda

erupted from the water and lunged toward its prey.

Lord Roxton aimed straight for its head but just as he fired, one of the beast's powerful coils knocked him over, spilling his ammunition into a tree behind the lunging predator, and slinging his rifle out of reach. Zambo quickly fired, as the serpent looped itself around the struggling calf, and even the iron spike to which they had fastened the calf's rope seemed to loosen from the ground toward the tugging force of the anaconda.

"He is a bit thick-skulled," shouted Zambo, re-loading his own gun.

"Oh, well, when all else fails," muttered Lord Roxton, leaping into the river. Almost instantly, snake, calf, and man disappeared, and the water stilled.

"The snake's not the only thick-skulled hunter in that river," sighed Zambo, taking aim at the temporarily quiet waters. "Come on, Lord Roxton. I know you . . . that thing hasn't beaten you yet. Come on . . . blast it, Roxton, where are you?"

"Onward, Christian soldiers!" exclaimed Lord Roxton, rising out of the water, holding the violently thrashing head of the snake by the jaws, which he held clamped shut.

"Praise the Lord," said Zambo with an exhausted sigh. "Keep it still!"

"You tellin' him or me?" exclaimed Lord Roxton, as the snake carried the two of them across a low forked branch overhanging the river.

"Use the fork! Quick, the fork!" Zambo shouted.

"What do you want me to do, shoot him or eat him?" replied Roxton indignantly.

"No, wedge his head in the fork of the branch!"

Roxton caught on immediately, and still wrestling against the twisting coils of the anaconda, rolled around and brought the two of them down through the fork of the large branch, where he was able to snag the thick neck of the snake in the jagged limb.

The hunter dropped down into the water, and Zambo threw him his gun. "You do the honors," Roxton's tall companion said with a grin.

"I almost feel sorry for it," he said, as he fired and the creature's thrashings slowed to a halt. "But I feel more sorry for the family of that fisherman he devoured last week. That won't be happening again."

Without warning, a cheer rose up from the shore. The villagers, who had evidently been watching the proceedings, ran forth and held Lord Roxton and Zambo up on their shoulders.

"Three cheers to St. George, Dragon-slayer!" they shouted. "Three cheers to St. Zambo, Dragon-slayer!"

"Congratulations, Lord Roxton," said the chief of the village. "You have slain the camoodi. We owe you our thanks."

"The glory belongs to God, for guiding my hands," replied Lord Roxton. "But I'm happy to be at your service, Chief Attalat."

"The beast was a curse to our people, and even in death the coals of its eyes burn with its hate," the chief said, scowling at the body, at which the children had already begun to throw rocks.

"I would imagine its eyes are phosphorescent, something like the firefly's method of attracting a mate," replied Lord Roxton.

"Surely you don't think there are more of them?" The chief looked out into the gloom uneasily.

"Oh, I have no doubt there are; some even bigger than this one," said Lord Roxton with a shrug. "I've heard stories from Lt. Col. Percy about one more than twice this size. But the instances of them attacking humans are rare, so I wouldn't worry. If another one shows up to cause a problem, we'll cope with it . . . just like we coped with that one there."

Zambo sat down on a log at the riverbank beside Lord Roxton. "I can't help thinking, Lord Roxton," said Zambo. "About that snake."

"What about it?"

"I don't think it was a little snake in the Garden of Eden that tempted Eve to taste the fruit."

"What, you think it was — one of those bigger beasties, like our friend here?" Lord Roxton tugged at his handlebar moustache thoughtfully. "What makes you say that?"

"Well, in the Garden, before Noah's flood, obviously . . ."

"Quite obviously."

"Obviously, things lived longer in those days, in a perfect environment, and since reptiles don't stop growing as long as they live . . ."

"I follow you so far, Zambo. Even people lived longer in those days. Perhaps a reptile in such an environment would grow to an enormous size. Is that what you're suggesting?"

"Well, naturally, God created man, and all the animals, full-grown, right?"

"Right."

"So wouldn't a serpent in the Garden of Eden, before the fall of man . . ."

"Lord Roxton!" came a cry from a canoe that was speeding toward them. "Lord Roxton! It's Maple White!" exclaimed the villager. "He's returned to the village, and badly injured! He needs your help! Please come at once!"

"Maple White!" exclaimed Zambo.

"I thought he was lost in the jungle, with Lt. Col. Percy and his men," said Lord Roxton.

Maple White was a missionary who had disappeared into the jungle years before, and, Lord Roxton knew, a faithful Christian. Lord Roxton had received some minimal medical training during his military service, so he and Zambo rushed to offer whatever assistance they could.

They found Maple White lying on a crude mattress inside a hut. He was an older gentleman, perhaps in his early sixties, with wild, white hair that seemed to sprout in every direction away from his face. His clothes were shredded around the edges, and he appeared to be, judging from his gaunt condition, suffering from starvation. Despite the hardships he had evidently endured, the wrinkles of his face curled into a gentle smile as Lord Roxton approached. "Lord Roxton! May God be praised that you are here," gasped Mr. White. He weakly handed over a tattered sketchbook. "Here, take this. It will show you . . . how to find a . . . a lost world. You'll find . . . there, living side by side . . . man . . . and . . . and . . . dinosaurs."

With that, Maple White breathed his last.

After the funeral, Lord Roxton and Zambo sat beside one another quietly.

"That is one man," said Lord Roxton, finally, "who I have no doubt that before the throne of judgement, our Lord will say, 'Well done, good and faithful servant. Enter into the joy of your Master's kingdom.'"

"As I am sure He will say of you, when your time comes," said Zambo.

"And the same of you, my friend." Lord Roxton drummed his fingers against the sketchbook. "I have no doubt of that whatever."

"Don't you think we should see what was in his sketchbook?" asked Zambo. "Evidently he spent his last strength in making certain we received it."

"Yeah, let's have a look," said Lord Roxton, dusting off the cover. "I'm a bit anxious to see what he meant by man and dinosaurs living side by side."

"That's not possible, is it?" said Zambo. "I thought dinosaurs died out long ago."

"Not nearly as long ago as the so-called scientists of the day would have us believe . . . if Mr. White knew what he was looking at."

Lord Roxton carefully opened the sketchbook, and peeled the water-stained pages apart, one by one.

"The first sketches don't seem very unusual," commented Lord Roxton. "Drawings of village huts, birds, and native people that Maple must have met on his journey are all I see so far."

"Wait!" interrupted Zambo. "There's the map he mentioned. If there's anything worth finding there, once we see what he . . ."

They both gasped in disbelief. For there, on the next wrinkled page, was a drawing that made Zambo and Lord Roxton's breath stop in their throats. It showed a native girl standing beside what looked like a fat, armored lizard with a tiny head and rows of diamond-shaped plates along its back. The most startling significance of this particular lizard, however, lay in its size. Judging from the girl in the sketch, it had to be well over 20 feet long, and 10 feet tall at the hip.

"What on earth is that?" Zambo wiped his forehead. "Is that a dinosaur, Lord Roxton?"

"Yep. Stegosaurus. I saw a model of one in the Crystal Palace exhibit, back in London," said Lord Roxton, as he carefully studied the picture. "Didn't have quite as many spikes on its tail as this one, though. And I would say this creature looks much more like I would expect a living dinosaur to look than those rather imaginative renditions I saw in England."

"Do you think the drawing is of a real, living animal?"

"God be praised," replied Lord Roxton. "Not only do I think so, but I sincerely believe there are more where this one came from, Zambo."

"The only way to prove that the drawings in Maple White's sketchbook are of living animals," said Lord Roxton, as he and Zambo paddled upriver, "is to find this mysterious 'Lost World' for ourselves, and photograph them. How much farther does the map show it to be?"

"Still a long way up the river and into the jungle," replied Zambo. "I just hope we have enough supplies, because the map is rather vague on distances. It seems to rely more heavily upon landmarks than the distances between them."

"I can understand that, easily enough," replied Lord Roxton. "It's hard to judge distances in the jungle, especially when moving through underbrush slows you down."

After many days on the river, they came to a tree resting at a peculiar angle on the water's edge. "Aha!" exclaimed Lord Roxton. "That's just the sign we were looking for. Look for where there are light green rushes instead of dark green undergrowth — that's the mouth of the stream into this Lost World."

"I can see how it could be so easily lost," muttered Zambo as he paddled up between the tall, thick weeds.

"Being so carefully hidden from mankind is the very thing that has preserved this world," replied Lord Roxton. "For I believe the so-called 'dragon-slayers' of the Middle Ages were in fact exterminating some of the last remaining dinosaurs, elsewhere on the globe."

Zambo and Lord Roxton paddled on into the stream for several days until they could go no farther, because the water had become too shallow for their canoe. They pulled it up onto the bank, and hid it among some shrubs, until they could return. After what seemed like weeks of traveling through the dark jungle and snake-infested swamps, they struggled up a rocky slope and saw before them a flat plain, covered with tree ferns. In the distance, rising out of the mist above the tree ferns, were the red cliffs of the huge plateau from Maple White's sketchbook.

"That, my good friend," Lord Roxton said in amazement, "must be the Lost World."

"Those cliffs must be over five hundred feet high!" exclaimed Zambo. "How are we going to get up there?"

"If Maple White was able to climb up there and draw the dinosaurs in his sketchbook, we'll manage our way up, too," explained Lord Roxton. They marched toward the plateau, their energy seemingly renewed now that they were in sight of their goal.

Late that afternoon they set up camp at the base of the cliffs. Lord Roxton had discovered a curious spire of rock standing away from the main plateau. Its top was level with that of its rocky neighbor, but separated by a gorge some 40 feet wide. A single tree stood at the top of this lonely mountain. Lord Roxton was getting out his camera to take a picture of this scene above them when a strange cry filled the air.

Zambo pointed at the tree atop the cliff. "Look, Lord Roxton! Coming out of the branches!"

Lord Roxton gasped in disbelief. Emerging from the branches above was what he could have only explained as a huge, sinister-looking pelican . . . without feathers. As the unusual creature spread its wings, Lord Roxton received a second shock. Its wings were not feathered either, but instead, looked to be leathery, almost batlike wings. All his years of hunting in the jungles around the globe could only lead him to one conclusion. It was some variety of pterosaur, which most scientists had thought extinct. Lord Roxton gathered his senses, and clicked the shutter on his camera before the creature flapped away.

"Zambo, we are on the edge of the greatest scientific discovery of this, or perhaps, any century," said Lord Roxton in amazement. "Finding so-called prehistoric creatures alive, and unchanged by any theories of mythical evolution. . . . Think of what awaits us just beyond those cliffs."

"Danger awaits us beyond those cliffs," said Zambo, pointing overhead.

Lord Roxton looked and groaned in disappointment, for gathering above them were storm clouds, pitch-black and already flashing forth with lightning.

"Cover that camera, at any cost!" warned Zambo. "Not only did our journey take longer than we expected, monsoon season has come early this year. This is only the first of the worst weather to come. We have to head back . . . or else we may not make it back alive."

Wearily, Lord Roxton agreed, as they hastily gathered their camping equipment. "Yes, Zambo, I believe the Royal Zoological Society in

London will be very interested in this photograph."

"Hopefully, they'll be willing to fund another, better-equipped expedition so we can make it up that cliff. Just think what we're leaving behind us," said Zambo, taking one last glance over his shoulder.

There was a flash of lightning, and seemingly in reply, a loud, trumpeting roar echoed across the countryside.

Lord Roxton and Zambo gazed inquisitively at one another as the rain began to fall.

The roar had come from the cliff above.

Chapter 2

Journalist

M any weeks later, a young man named Edward Malone was heading over to the house of his girlfriend, Gladys Hungerton, not far
from Lord Roxton's home in London. This was not just any visit, for
today Edward intended to propose to her. He wanted her to be his wife.

As he entered her living room, he got down on one knee. But before
he could say anything, Gladys shook her head in disapproval.
"Oh, Edward. Please don't ruin our friendship by
proposing marriage to me. It's so much
nicer this way."

"But, why not?" exclaimed
Edward. "Is there something
wrong with me?"

"It's your character,"
she said.

"I can change, if
only you'll give me
the chance,"
Edward
pleaded. "I
must have

19

you as my wife. What must I do to please you?"

"The ideal man I'm looking for would not speak like that. He would be a sterner man, not so ready to adapt himself to the whim of a silly girl. No, Edward . . . I'm looking for a husband I can be proud of. An adventurer, a great sportsman, like that dashing Lord Roxton."

"The big-game hunter?" Edward scratched his head. "We can't all be adventurers. A junior reporter like myself hardly has a chance."

"But there are chances all around you," argued Gladys. "There are heroisms all around us waiting to be done. When I marry, I want to marry a man of adventure."

Edward sighed. "You deserve such a man. Very well; I'll go ask my editor, Mr. McArdle, for an adventurous assignment."

Gladys looked at Edward with a bit more interest in her eyes. "I'm glad to see our little talk has had such an effect on you."

"And after I've survived an adventure?" Edward asked eagerly.

"Not another word until then. Now, hurry. You're late for work."

— — — —

Edward hurried into the office of the *London Daily Gazette*, to see his editor, Mr. McArdle. "Well, Mr. Malone, I very much enjoyed your copy on the Southwark fire. Keep up the good work," said Mr. McArdle. "Now what can I do for you?"

"Well, sir, I need a mission with adventure and danger in it."

"You seem quite anxious to lose your life," Mr. McArdle said warily. "As good as your work has been, the reporters who have been with us longer usually get those sort of assignments. And adventure, anyhow . . . in this modern world, is an endangered thing. The big blank spaces on the map are all being filled in. Wait! Blank spaces on the map! That's it! What about exposing a fraud?"

"I don't see how that would . . ." Edward began.

"A fraud with a potentially dangerous bodyguard?" Mr. McArdle grinned.

"That would be at least something, sir. What's his name?" asked Edward.

"Have you ever heard of Lord George Roxton?"

"Lord George Roxton!" exclaimed Edward. "The famous adventurer? Isn't he the fellow who assaulted that reporter from the *Telegraph?*"

"No, no," Mr. McArdle replied, waving his hands. "Lord Roxton is a good Christian man. He's not the violent type. But his man Austin — his bodyguard and butler — is overprotective of him. Didn't you say it was adventure you're after?"

"Well, sir, obviously, I thank you for anything you can give me, but . . ."

"Here's all you should need," interrupted Mr. McArdle, handing Edward a slip of paper. "He lives in Enmore Park. He went to South America some time ago, started some nonsense about prehistoric animals. Even claims to have a photograph, supposedly faked. Very touchy on the subject. I imagine it's some sort of publicity stunt for his next expedition. You would probably best get on his good side by posing as a theology student interested in zoology — two of his biggest interests. You studied to be a minister at first, didn't you?"

"Well, until my parents were killed," Edward answered sadly. "I just sort of lost interest in the subject after that."

"I'm sorry to hear about that," McArdle said. He tapped his chin thoughtfully. "Well, Mr. Malone, Roxton is your man, so off you run to see what you can make of him. You're a big enough fellow to look after yourself. Anyway, all of our reporters are safe. Employer's Liability Act, you see. We're covered for any damages." Mr. McArdle pushed Edward outside his office and slammed the door.

"Damages?" Malone gulped.

After Malone had studied the paper Mr. McArdle had given him, he decided the best way to meet Lord Roxton was to write him a letter. Unfortunately, it was a dishonest letter. Edward was willing to do anything for an adventure, so he could marry Gladys.

He started to write.

Dear Lord Roxton,

As a humble student of theology (with a minor in zoology), the results of your recent trip to South America have been of particular interest to me. I was recently studying the notes of your comments at the last lecture of the esteemed Professor Summerlee, and your opinion toward his endorsement of Darwin's theory of evolution seem, I dare to say, a bit harsh on the man. Are you certain, in light of modern science and research, that you do not wish to modify your statements? Who is to say that evolution may not be the method through which God creates? I feel that there must be some middle ground on which science and religion can agree, and I have viewpoints that could only be elaborated upon in a personal discussion. With your kind consent, I request the honor of calling upon you at 11 o'clock this Wednesday.

With all due respect, I thank you for the opportunity to meet you.

Sincerely,
Edward D. Malone

Despite the closing comments, the letter was anything but sincere. The letter bothered Edward's conscience, but he had it delivered all the same. Two days later he received a reply.

Enmore Park, W.

Sir, I have received your note, and I must admit I find your readiness to accept popular theory as proven fact disturbing. However, this seems to be an unfortunately widespread practice, so I cannot say that it catches me fully by surprise. I must say, therefore, if you truly believe that (well, shall we say) imaginative statement regarding evolution being 'the method through which God creates,' then we are in serious need of an interview (at the day and hour you suggested).

Kindly present this letter to my butler, Austin, who must take every precaution in shielding me from those intrusive rascals that our society refers to as 'journalists.'

Yours faithfully,
Lord George Roxton.

Edward was not proud of the method by which he had won his interview, but he had it. With a heavy sigh, he headed over to the home of Lord Roxton and knocked at the door.

A tall, hulking butler answered the door. Edward could not help thinking that he looked like the resulting experiment from Mary Shelley's novel *Frankenstein*. A thin, white hairline receded from over a low, furrowed brow. Small eyes within puckered sockets beheld Edward suspiciously.

"Expected?" asked the butler.

"Yes, an appointment," replied Edward.

"Your letter?" The man held out his massive hand, and took the letter. He glanced over it quickly, and nodded. "Right," he said, and stepped aside for Edward to enter. As the butler closed the door, a small attractive woman, neatly dressed, joined them in the hallway.

"One moment, young man," said the woman. "Thank you, Austin," she said to the butler. "I'll take it from here."

"Very good, madam," said Austin, and stepped back down the hallway. As the large man stomped down the hallway, Edward shuddered. He hoped that he wouldn't be evicted from the premises by a bodyguard that size!

"May I ask you — Mr. Malone, is it?" asked the small woman politely.

"Yes ma'am."

"Nice to meet you, Mr. Malone. I am Miss Victoria Roxton, Lord Roxton's sister. I must ask you, Mr. Malone, have you ever met my brother before?" she asked.

"No madam, I have not had that honor," Edward replied.

Miss Roxton smiled patiently at Edward. "I do trust you do not wish to ask him about . . . South America?"

Edward could not lie to a lady. "I'm afraid so."

"Oh, dear, that's the most touchy subject of them all," she said, shaking her head as they headed up the stairs to Lord Roxton's study. "Well, then, whatever you do, pretend to believe him. At first I thought it was a tall tale, but whatever happened to him in that jungle, I've found that he believes the story himself. A more honest man has never lived. He's a good Christian man, and couldn't lie to me if his life depended on it. I love my brother dearly," she added with a sigh. "I just wish those awful journalists would leave him alone. Austin, bless his heart — has gotten into trouble, as you may have heard, removing them from the premises. Doesn't know his own strength. Well, you shouldn't have to worry about that."

Edward grinned and chuckled weakly as Miss Roxton knocked on the door. "George, Mr. Malone is here to see you!"

"Come in, Mr. Malone, come in!" came the friendly greeting from within the study. Miss Roxton opened the door for Edward as he stepped in, and she closed the door behind him. Sitting behind the desk in the dimly lit study was Lord Roxton, dressed in a white suit, with his feet propped up in front of him. "Have a seat, young-fellah-m'lad," he said. "Don't look so shy; I've been expecting you."

"I have an appointment," Edward said nervously, and placed the envelope upon the desk. "I've very much enjoyed reading of your adventures, sir. Well, except for the last . . ."

Lord Roxton winced as if in pain. "Yes, well, as you know, I generally don't like to discuss that last little tale. Reporters, eh? Lord forgive 'em. But enough about that.

"So you are the young man who thinks God creates through evolution. Dear me, what have the seminaries of this new century produced? If it could have been spoken more simply in the Book of Genesis, young-fellah-m' lad, I simply don't know how. God created everything . . . including mankind . . . in six days . . . six literal days. Then he rested on the seventh. You see, my young friend, whenever we start to leave things open to popular interpretation, we're setting ourselves up for trouble. Don't you agree?"

"Sir, I am obviously a mere sophomore in theology," stuttered Edward.

"Ah, then, you have surely learned your Scripture, and how it would reflect upon this discussion," Lord Roxton said with a sly grin.

"Uh . . . surely," Edward said nervously.

"For instance, what it says in Matthew 27:5."

"Naturally," said Edward.

"And, in the latter half of Luke 10:37" said Lord Roxton.

"Obviously," said Edward, having no idea what was written in either half of either verse.

"But," continued Lord Roxton in a gentle voice, "what does that prove?"

"Yes," said Edward. "What does that prove?"

"It proves," said Lord Roxton with a weary sigh, "that I am never going to get any peace in my private life from nosy journalists like yourself. Know your Scripture indeed!"

"What, uh, what was that Scripture?" asked Edward, backing toward the door.

Lord Roxton quietly stepped over to a cord dangling from the ceiling, and pulled it, triggering a bell. "Matthew 27:5 says 'Judas went out and hanged himself.' And then, in Luke 10:37 'go and do likewise.' "

Edward reached behind him for the door handle and backed farther against the door. "Look here, sir," he said. "I shall not be assaulted."

"Oh, don't be ridiculous, young man," Lord Roxton said. "I don't wish for anyone in my home to be assaulted. I'm just going to have you escorted outside."

"I won't stand for it, Lord . . ." Edward began to say, and surely enough, he was not standing much longer, for he suddenly found himself lifted from the floor by one of Austin's heavy hands.

"Now, Austin, be gentle with him," said Lord Roxton. "We can't have you getting into any more trouble for mistreating our guests . . . even the unwelcome ones."

"Yes, Lord Roxton," said Austin sheepishly, carrying the struggling Edward downstairs. Austin opened the front door with one hand, still holding Edward aloft with the other at the top of the stairs. "Do pop by again and see us, Mr. Malone," muttered Austin.

He released Edward, who rolled down the front stairs, and finally to a dusty stop at the sidewalk. "What's all this, then?" demanded a voice. Edward looked up to see a policeman standing over him. "At it again, I see, Austin," said the policeman as he took out his notebook. "Do you hold charges against him for assaulting you, young man?"

"No," Edward said. "I won't hold charges. It was my fault. I intruded on his master. He was just doing his job."

"Very well," said the surprised policeman, as he prepared to leave. "But let's not have such goings-on any more, shall we, Austin?"

"Come along inside, young man," said a voice from above, after the policeman left. Edward looked up to see Lord Roxton leaning out his study window. "Apparently I'm not done with our little visit yet."

Astonished, Austin opened the door to allow Edward (who looked even more bewildered than the butler) inside. Austin closed the door behind him.

Chapter 3

Confidential

M iss Roxton rushed up to Austin. "Austin, you should be ashamed of yourself for treating that nice young man so brutally, and . . . Oh! Here he is!"

Lord Roxton, appearing at the top of the stairs above them, agreed. "Yes, here he is. But not a student, as he would have us believe; rather a journalist. And we are going upstairs to continue our discussion in, I trust, a more civilized manner. Mr. Malone and I must discuss South America, and must not be disturbed, Victoria."

"You're inviting a journalist to discuss . . . South America? Yes. Very well, George."

"I do apologize for deceiving you, madam," said Malone as he followed Lord Roxton to his study, where he closed the door and they sat down.

"Now we are going to talk about South America," said Lord Roxton. "No interruptions, if you please. First of all, nothing I say will be repeated in your newspaper, nor in any public way, without my express permission. Do I make myself clear?"

"You have my word of honor, sir," said Edward.

"The honor of a journalist," Lord Roxton muttered with a chuckle. "Very well, that will have to do. You have expressed honor, in the face of authority, and that is why I invited you back in. Among your profession, this was the first evidence of honor I have ever seen expressed, and I commend that heartily, young-fellah-m'lad. I am very impressed, and I believe that you should be rewarded for your behavior. And your reward is simply what you came for.

"Here is what you came to hear in the first place. Some time ago, I went to the Amazon on a missionary expedition, after hearing stories about so-called 'prehistoric survivors,' in hopes that reported stories of such would continue to confirm God's creation, and to cast the inescapable spotlight of doubt upon the evolution myth. I must pause here to ask you, despite your earlier dishonest episode — are you, young fella, a Christian?"

"I'm afraid I used to be, sir," admitted Malone, "until my parents, who were missionaires, were killed by a tribe they went to evangelize. I felt a loving God would not have allowed that to happen, and thus I consider myself an agnostic."

"Someone who doesn't know why he believes what he believes," Lord Roxton said, with a patient smile. "Young-fellah-m'lad, I simply do not believe it is possible to lose your salvation. Either you were perhaps not a Christian in the first place, or you are simply in a state of doubt now. That's a natural reaction to a tragedy. Despite the admirable efforts of parents, we do not become Christians through osmosis . . . we don't absorb it from others. It's a result of a personal acceptance of Christ. Our parents can't do that for us. And I do express my condolences for your parents. I have done extensive work with missionaries myself, and, well, I cannot explain how the Lord works in His mysterious ways or why bad things can and often do happen to very good people. I can only say that I hope this tale will reaffirm the faith you once knew."

"While I cannot make such a promise, I am very interested to hear your story," said Edward.

"Your case then, is not hopeless." Lord Roxton continued, "During my travels along the Amazon river, I was called to the deathbed of Maple White, the missionary. He had emerged from the jungle after being thought lost for years. My faithful companion Zambo and I were honored to be with him in his last moments, when he presented this to me."

Lord Roxton handed Edward the sketchbook and opened it to the page with the dinosaur drawings. Edward looked doubtful. "He could have easily seen these in a textbook, you realize."

"Did you notice the drawing of the cliffs, the lonely mountain of rock, and the tree atop it?" inquired Lord Roxton. As Edward nodded, the hunter handed him a photograph, which showed the exact same scene, but closer, and from a slightly different angle.

"That's definitely the same place," admitted Edward. "At least the cliffs and the trees exist, and . . . wait a minute. What's that strange-looking bird sitting in the tree?"

Lord Roxton grinned with satisfaction. "Some have called it an ugly, oversized pelican."

"That's what I would say," Edward agreed, shuddering.

"I cannot, I fear, congratulate you upon your eyesight," Lord Roxton said. "But I ask you to examine this textbook, and to kindly concentrate on the illustration of this flying reptile, and please disregard the nonsense about when it supposedly lived."

Edward looked at the illustration and compared it with the photograph. "It certainly has to be more than a coincidence. But what about the dinosaur in the drawing?"

"I can only assume that Mr. White somehow made it up onto the plateau, where the flying creature disappeared. Therefore, we can rest assured that there is a way up, somehow. And we are going to find it."

"We? The two of us? How?" Edward asked eagerly.

"More than two of us. We are going to the Royal Zoological Society tonight to endure another lecture of Professor Summerlee, a somewhat, eh," Lord Roxton scratched his neck, trying to come up with a polite way to phrase it, "long-winded evolutionist. I simply don't have the funds to make such a trip, but his lectures are popular with the public, and he is thus quite wealthy. He will fund the trip."

"But isn't he one of those who called you a fraud?" asked Edward. "Why should he fund an expedition for us?"

"Young man, you will realize as you get older, that you can be sneaky without being dishonest. I will meet you at 8 o'clock this evening at the Royal Zoological Society. I will be upon the platform, and you will know what to say when the time comes."

"But how will I —"

"Just trust that the Lord will lead you to say the right thing at the right time. I know, you think he doesn't listen to you, but he does. I will pray for you in the meantime. Good day."

With that, Lord Roxton gently pushed Edward out of his study.

Confused, Edward left, very much looking forward to the lecture that evening.

Chapter 4

Lecture

A t the Royal Zoological Society, Edward sat down in the audience, and waited for the lecture to begin. He saw an empty seat on the speaker's platform and guessed that Lord Roxton was to sit there and had not yet arrived. Professor Summerlee, a tall, thin man in his late sixties, strode to the podium, to the delight of the audience. "Thank you, ladies and gentlemen," said Professor Summerlee. "It overjoys me to see that the general public, in their enthusiasm for education and in their quest for enlightenment, has come to my humble lecture this evening. Some have claimed the earth to be merely thousands of years old, created by God in seven days. Well, our modern science is beginning to show us that that isn't quite how it happened, which I shall discuss briefly. Our main subject tonight, however, is that great source of public excitement . . . dinosaurs!"

As Edward wrote as quickly as he could in his notebook, he noted how the audience treated Professor Summerlee with royal respect. The man's position in the public eye had brought him as close to being a celebrity as a scientist could hope to become. Glancing past the lecturer, however, Edward saw that Lord Roxton was quietly sitting down. Edward waved, and Lord Roxton nodded with a knowing grin.

"Though their skeletal remains may frighten us in our natural history museums, we can rest assured that our ancestors were never in any danger from these creatures, for fossil evidence shows conclusively that these frightful creatures were quite fortunately extinct long before mankind ever made his footprints upon this planet."

"Question!" exclaimed Lord Roxton, and it so startled Professor Summerlee that he dropped his glasses. Not used to interruptions, he quietly turned around and could not conceal a scowl in Lord Roxton's direction.

He turned back to the audience and smiled. "I see," said Professor Summerlee, "that it is my — uh, my good friend Lord Roxton, the adventurer. As I was saying . . ."

"Question!" boomed Lord Roxton once more.

Professor Summerlee turned once more to face his rival. "This is really intolerable," snarled Professor Summerlee. "I must request, Lord Roxton, that you cease your unmannerly interruptions!"

Lord Roxton rose to stand beside Professor Summerlee at the podium. "And I must ask you in turn, Professor Summerlee, to kindly cease your public assertions that do not quite align with scientific fact. You seem to be mistaking popular scientific theory for *fact*. A common enough mistake, but one that I had hoped would be beneath a man of your achievements. I believe, in fact, that the fossil record you mentioned has not yet shown conclusively that dinosaurs were extinct before man's appearance on God's green earth."

One of Professor Summerlee's supporters on the platform rose to defend him. "Lord Roxton, let's discuss these personal views later, please!"

"Oh, why not discuss them now?" Lord Roxton inquired, and stood at the podium. "Ladies and gentlemen, I do beg your forgiveness on behalf of our speaker, Professor Summerlee, whose imaginative history of life upon our planet has no doubt caused confusion among you. Indeed, Professor Summerlee's appearance alone has provided the closest thing to evidence I have ever beheld for apelike ancestry."

"Really, sir, the very idea!" snapped Professor Summerlee.

"All levity aside, my good people, I do not wish to allow this lecture to be a personal attack, and for that last remark, Professor Summerlee, I do sincerely apologize. I cannot blame you for resenting my interruptions. I am the first to admit my membership in this fine organization is an honorary one, and I do not wish to treat that honor lightly. Tonight, I hope to give an extreme display of will over emotion. I simply mean to put forth a challenge of our lecturer's accuracy on the point of so-called extinction of certain animal life upon our planet."

"And I suppose you have seen some of these prehistoric animals yourself, Lord Roxton," said Professor Summerlee, sarcastically.

"I have," said Lord Roxton, at which the audience began to laugh.

Professor Summerlee, waved his hands to quiet the crowd down. "Please, ladies and gentlemen, this should be educational for us all. If not at least . . . entertaining," he added with a sneer. "Do go on, Lord Roxton."

"Creatures which were supposed to be of the Triassic, and Jurassic, and even Cretaceous eras — monsters which could easily devour our largest, so-called modern mammals — still exist in isolation. They exist on an isolated plateau where they have, since Noah's flood, lived side by side with mankind. Unchanged and unevolved. I have presented photographic evidence, which has been refused as fakery. What will it take to convince this audience?"

"I think a live specimen would be impossible to fake," suggested Professor Summerlee.

"Then under such conditions, my reputation as an honest man would be restored?" asked Lord Roxton.

"Undoubtedly," said Summerlee. "Not only will I be the first in line for an autographed copy of your adventures, but I will personally offer you a public apology for our, uh . . . foolishness, if you provide us with a live specimen of dinosaur life."

"Then I shall put you to the test, Summerlee. Will you appoint a representative from the members of the Zoological Society on this platform on an expedition — to test my claims, and to find and return with a living dinosaur?"

"I will do better than that, Lord Roxton," said Summerlee. "I will go myself."

After the audience had finished cheering, Lord Roxton continued. "Then I will place in your hands such material necessary to make your way to this hidden plateau in South America. However, as you are going to test the accuracy of my statements, I will request someone accompanies you to verify your statements. Do I have any volunteers from the audience?"

At that moment Edward found himself standing up, much to his own surprise. It was as if he had not even stood with his own strength.

Lord Roxton smiled. "Ah, it seems we have a volunteer. Young man, tell everyone your name, please."

"My name is Edward D. Malone. I'm a reporter for the *London Daily Gazette*."

"Ah, a reporter. Very good," said Summerlee. "That should add some weight to the evidence we find, or rather — don't find. And look, we seem to have another volunteer."

Much to Lord Roxton's surprise, there was a man standing a few seats in front of Edward. "My name is Sir Arthur Conan Doyle," said the man, "and most of you are familiar with my adventures of Sherlock Holmes. My interest in such unusual adventures, as you all well know, is extensive. While Mr. Malone reports the facts for his paper, I would be happy to report more in-depth accounts of our exploits, in serialized format, for *Strand Magazine*. My former profession as a doctor might also come in handy on such a dangerous mission."

"In this case, I suggest," said Lord Roxton, "that both of these gentlemen are elected, with Professor Summerlee's kind approval, to accompany Professor Summerlee upon his journey to investigate, and, I trust, to report the truth of my earlier statements."

Professor Summerlee agreed, and with the audience applauding, the meeting was at an end. As Edward walked out into the street, he felt someone tap his shoulder. He turned to see the gentleman who had introduced himself at the meeting as Sir Arthur Conan Doyle. Malone thought the famous author, grinning from behind his bristly moustache, bore more than a passing resemblance to his character, Dr. Watson. "Mr. Malone, we are to be companions, eh?" Sir Arthur said with a friendly laugh. "Perhaps you and Lord Roxton could spare me half an hour, for there are a couple of things we need to discuss."

Sir Arthur Conan Doyle was an unusual man, to say the least.

He had gained fame years before as the creator of the famed London detective, Sherlock Holmes, and his assistant Dr. Watson, and their shared adventures did very well with the public. At first.

By the year 1910, it was evident that Mr. Holmes (and his creator) needed some rest. The unmistakable evidence came in the form of a novel entitled *Sherlock Holmes Loses His Keys*. It was such a miserable failure that the publisher, after two embarrassing weeks of attempted sales, denied any knowledge that the book ever existed. Indeed, any recorded existence of the book ever being written has generally been withheld from the public, and it has been politely ignored in lists of Sir Arthur Conan Doyle's works.

Doyle needed a hit that would recapture the past successes of Sherlock Holmes' original adventures.

But where could he find a source of adventure that would be a hit with the public?

Dinosaurs were enjoying yet another surge of popularity. Their mighty towering figures that dwarfed the modern elephants stretched several stories high into the yawning expanses of museums, bewildering the public that anything so huge could support its own weight.

Rumor had it that the American illustrator and animator, Winsor McCay, author-illustrator of the popular comic strip *Little Nemo in Slumberland*, was working on an animated dinosaur film. *Gertie the Dinosaur*, the working title of this film, would be taken on the vaudeville circuit by McCay himself, upon its completion. The public could not wait to see it, but due to the expensive and time-consuming process of early animation (not to mention the fact that McCay alone would make all the animation drawings himself) they would have to wait some time.

Doyle decided he would very much enjoy writing an adventure with dinosaurs, but he needed inspiration. His inspiration came in the form of a story run in the *London Daily Gazette*: "62-foot-long Snake Killed on the Amazon! Could This Be a Prehistoric Survivor?"

When Doyle heard rumors that Lord Roxton, one of the men responsible for killing the giant anaconda, might be speaking at the next meeting of the Royal Zoological Society, he wasted no time in making arrangements to attend.

Not only was he not disappointed, he was delighted to discover he might get to see living dinosaurs himself.

Doyle knew, from personal experience, that the greatest adventure stories were written by those who had actually lived them.

Edward followed Lord Roxton and Sir Arthur to the home of the famous writer, and they sat down, admiring the many handsomely bound volumes of the Sherlock Holmes adventures. "I was in South America some time ago," Sir Arthur explained, "and I don't doubt that every word of what Lord Roxton says is true. The Amazon jungle is a place I dearly love — one of the few areas left where a man can have true adventure. I hope you don't mind adventure, young man, for that's exactly what we're in for."

"That's why I came along on this trip," explained Edward. "My girlfriend won't marry me until I've survived an adventure."

"While I don't agree with your motives, I do appreciate the spirit behind them," said Lord Roxton. "This journey will no doubt educate you on several points. One is the wonder of God's creation on this green earth . . . especially in the Amazon. The more you know of that particular country, young-fellah-m'lad, the more you'll know anything is possible there. Anything. In this world, there are just a few narrow waterlanes folk travel; outside that is darkness. Just because somebody slapped a name on it on a map doesn't mean it's been thoroughly explored."

"I'm willing to be a part of that exploration," Sir Arthur offered. "I understand that you have done a bit of exploration there yourself?"

"Oh, sure, bits here and there," replied Lord Roxton. "But don't think venomous snakes and oversized lizards are the only dangers we're likely to encounter. There are dangerous men in that country as well. Why, five years ago, I waged my own little war of personal justice on the Putomayo River. There was a villainous slave-murderer, the king of them all, Pedro Lopez. He won't be terrorizing the poor blokes of that country anymore."

"If I survive this adventure, Gladys will surely marry me," Edward said, with an uneasy gulp.

"Well, that's true," said Lord Roxton with a chuckle. "If you survive."

Edward laughed nervously. Lord Roxton had a peculiar sense of humor.

Chapter 5

Manaus

A s they boarded the boat to leave England, Edward was astonished to hear that Lord Roxton wasn't going to accompany them on their journey. Though he pleaded with the man, Lord Roxton's mind seemed to be made up. "Truth is truth," he said, "and nothing that is reported on this journey will affect it, anyway. Your instructions to find your way are in this sealed envelope. I entrust it to you, Mr. Malone, that you will open this envelope in the village of Manaus on the Amazon, at the date, hour, and location marked on the outside. Do you understand?"

Edward nodded sadly. "What will you allow me to write for the newspaper?"

"Since the publication of facts is the object of your journey, I will not place any limits upon letters to your editor, except for any specific locations. Goodbye, Mr. Malone. You have placed in me some hope for your profession. And goodbye, Sir Arthur. I congratulate you in advance for the novel of a lifetime that awaits you."

"Goodbye, Lord Roxton," said Sir Arthur. "I am sorely disappointed you won't be joining us. Your reputation as an adventurer precedes you, and I would have loved to witness your exploits firsthand. It would have been invaluable to my story."

"And goodbye, Professor Summerlee," said Lord Roxton. "If

you are yet capable of self-improvement, you will certainly return to London a wiser — and more humble man."

Before Professor Summerlee could utter a sarcastic remark, Lord Roxton turned and disappeared into the crowd that waved farewell to the departing passengers.

After crossing the Atlantic Ocean they made their way by steamship up the Amazon to the village of Manaus. In the sitting room of their hotel, Sir Arthur, Professor Summerlee, and Edward met just before the appointed hour, and set the envelope on the table in front of them while the last few minutes ticked away. The slight squeak of the ceiling fan above was the only sound that disturbed the silence of their anticipation. Soon their journey into the dark jungle would begin, and they would be witnessing the largest, most magnificent reptiles of God's creation. Each squeak of the fan seemed to denote the tick of another second on the grandfather clock behind their wicker chairs. "We've seven minutes left," said Sir Arthur, glancing at the envelope eagerly. "The old chap is quite precise."

Professor Summerlee took the envelope with a sarcastic grin and fanned himself with it. "I have better business to attend to than running about, disproving the theories of a madman. Let's open it now."

"Now, now, let's play this game according to the rules," said Sir Arthur. "It is by Lord Roxton's goodwill that we're here, and it would be bad form to not follow instructions to the letter."

Professor Summerlee sighed and replaced the envelope on the table for the remaining minutes. Although the electric fans above and the shade trees outside the window kept the room considerably cooler than the hot, muggy streets in front of the hotel, beads of sweat began to trickle down Edward's forehead. What if they couldn't follow Lord Roxton's directions? What if they got lost in the jungle, and fell prey to the cannibals he had heard stories about? Without Lord Roxton's personal direction, how could the expedition hope to succeed? Much to his relief, his thoughts were finally interrupted when the old grandfather clock wearily struck the hour, and Sir Arthur opened the letter.

He gasped in dismay.

The sheet of paper was blank!

Sir Arthur turned the sheet over, and still, there was nothing written on it.

"Perhaps it's written in invisible ink," suggested Edward.

Sir Arthur held up the paper to the light. "It's no use, my young friend," said Sir Arthur. "I'm certain nothing has ever been written on this paper!"

"May I come in?" inquired a voice from the shadows. "You fellas seem to be in need of some guidance."

"Lord Roxton!" exclaimed Edward.

"I must apologize for the small ruse I played upon you in the part of the envelope," said Lord Roxton, "but I had other business to attend to. I feared I would have endured unwelcome pressure to travel out with you."

"Not from me, sir," snarled Professor Summerlee, crumpling the envelope in his wrinkled fist.

"Is all ready for our journey?" asked Lord Roxton.

"We can start tomorrow," said Sir Arthur. "I've chartered a steamship to carry us as far upstream as possible, and then we'll have to brave the smaller streams by canoe the rest of the way. I was a bit concerned, at first, but then we found someone who has made the journey before. Someone, I believe, you'll remember. Ah, here he is now!"

"Zambo!" exclaimed Lord Roxton, rushing forth to shake his

friend's hand. "How good to see you!"

"Lord Roxton, again the Lord has blessed us with one another's company," said Zambo. "This time we shall not be stopped by the rainy season. And this time, knowing we have such a long journey ahead of us, we are better prepared. I have hired men to help us carry our provisions."

The next day they set out on their journey. The sun shone over the numerous palm trees and down onto the docks of the massive river, which was bustling with preparations for the day's two primary activities: fishing, and transporting goods and travelers to their destinations along the countless tributaries of the huge Amazon water system. Lord Roxton and his companions met with the men who were to be their porters, who carried supplies. One of the men seemed to know Lord Roxton. "Lord Roxton, I have heard so much about you!" said the man named Gomez. "The tale of how you freed the slaves from Pedro Lopez is a legend among our people."

"I am afraid there are mixed feelings about my war against Lopez among your people as well," replied Lord Roxton. "The slaves were happy to be free, but those who wished to exploit them, well, they weren't too happy with me."

"Ah, si, si," said Gomez. "You are very true in speaking so."

Gomez gave Lord Roxton a curious, lingering smile as he continued to load their supplies onto the ship.

Zambo leaned over to Lord Roxton's ear. "There's something familiar about that fellow, but I can't be sure."

"I know what you mean," replied Lord Roxton, slowly. "It's like I've seen him somewhere before, but for the life of me, I can't imagine where."

Soon they were unloading their supplies from the steamship and onto the two canoes that would bear them through the remaining treacherous waterways. It was not long before they discovered that Lord Roxton's warning about dangerous men being in South America was true. As they paddled through the waters, they began to hear drums.

"Can you tell what those drums mean, Zambo?" asked Lord Roxton. "Can't mean any good, from the sound of 'em."

"I know only that they are war drums, but that is all that I can say for certain," replied Zambo, increasing the rate of his paddling. "We would do well to move as quickly through these parts as possible."

"I know exactly what they say," said Gomez, hiding beneath a blanket, as he shuddered in fear. "The drums say, they kill us if they can . . . kill us if they can."

They prepared for an attack that night, anchoring their canoes in midstream with heavy rocks, but no attack came. The next day, as they neared the rapids, the drums stopped. This was fortunate, because the rapids were too dangerous to travel; they had to pick up their canoes on the bank and walk around the treacherous water. After the river became safe to travel upon again, they returned their canoes to its surface. It was not long before Lord Roxton let out a cry of joy, pointing to a familiar tree. "There it is — our landmark!" he shouted. "Now look for the light green rushes among the dark green undergrowth . . . that's the mouth of the stream into our Lost World."

Going into their secret passageway, soon the water once more became too shallow for the canoes, which the porters hid for them among the bushes. Again, Lord Roxton found himself braving the dark jungle and the snake-infested swamps until at last, after many, many days, he and his companions, on the brink of exhaustion, climbed the rocky slope and saw before them the flat plain, covered with tree ferns.

"Take a look at that, Professor Summerlee," said Lord Roxton, confidently.

The usually sarcastic Summerlee had a look of sheer wonder on his face, as did the rest of the travelers. In the distance, rising out of the mist above the tree ferns, were the familiar red cliffs of Maple White's sketchbook plateau. "That's a good five hundred feet or more to climb," said Sir Arthur, looking through his binoculars.

"Look at that!" shouted Lord Roxton, pointing excitedly ahead. What looked like a huge bird flapped slowly up from among the tree ferns and disappeared in the distance near the cliffs. "Did you see that? Summerlee, did you see?"

"I saw something. What do you claim it was?" Summerlee inquired skeptically.

"To my best judgement, I would say a pterosaur," replied Lord Roxton.

Summerlee laughed. "A ptero-fiddlestick! That was a stork, if I ever saw one."

Lord Roxton slung his backpack over his shoulder after a patient shrug, and continued to march. Sir Arthur leaned over to Edward as they neared the plateau. "I focused my binoculars on it just before it cleared the trees. I'm no zoologist, but I'll stake my reputation that wasn't any bird I've ever seen."

That evening, Lord Roxton had shot an ajouti (a small, pig-like animal) that Zambo began to prepare for their supper. "At last," muttered Professor Summerlee, rubbing his hands together, "a decent meal in this God-forsaken country."

"Here, now, I thought you were an atheist, Professor Summerlee," said Lord Roxton with a grin. "Good to hear you at least making a reference to the existence of God. Maybe there's hope for you yet."

"My dear Lord Roxton, whatever life we find upon that cliff shall have to be very impressive indeed to prove to me the existence of any supreme, intelligent being," Professor Summerlee informed his companion with a condescending glare. "Why, as far as I'm concerned, I would be more ready to believe God's existence if I were suddenly overtaken by a bat-winged demon than if we . . ."

Suddenly, a horrible shriek filled the air, and they heard the flapping of leathery wings. Everyone dived into the trees in fear as a tremendous, winged shadow swooped down into their camp and snatched their supper from where it rested over the fire. It flapped up to the craggy peak where the tree stood, and roosted. They could see the full moon behind its almost transparent wings as they spread, carrying the creature back over the cliffs to disappear behind the rim of the plateau overhead.

Lord Roxton stepped out of the woods, smiling. "I think that Professor Summerlee can at least admit that the pterosaur — the photographic specimen I showed him before our journey — has just dropped in for dinner. Of course, Professor Summerlee will understand that when I speak of a pterosaur I mean a stork — only it is the kind of stork which has no feathers, a leathery skin, membranous wings, and teeth in its jaws."

Professor Summerlee sighed meekly. "Lord Roxton, I owe you an apology, sir. I have been very much in the wrong, and I beg you to forget what is past."

After a bewildered moment of beholding Professor Summerlee's outstretched hand, Lord Roxton at last took hold of it and shook it firmly, smiling. "I appreciate and accept your apology, Professor Summerlee. We must now lay the matter to rest, for tomorrow we ascend into the Lost World!"

When they arose the next morning and attempted to ascend the plateau, however, they were in for a shock. Maple White's directions led them to a cave where there was supposed to be a secret passage up onto the plateau. As they were standing there, getting their gear ready to go inside, a large boulder tumbled down from the cliffs above. Lord Roxton, who was nearest the cave, just missed being struck by the huge rock which now blocked the entrance. They were going to have to find another way up.

After circling the plateau, a lengthy march of well over 22 miles, they eventually came back to rest in their base camp. They had seen no possible way up. It looked hopeless.

The next morning, they were all awakened by a shout of joy from Sir Arthur's tent. "Gentlemen, the solution to our ascension, as Mr. Holmes would say, is elementary!" he said. "The problem is solved."

"You've found a way up?" asked Lord Roxton.

"I venture to think so. While we see that the cliffs of the plateau slope outward, climbing in that manner would prove futile. However, if you'll follow me up the plateau's neighbor, I believe I can show you the problem to be much less complicated than we had at first anticipated."

Lord Roxton followed Sir Arthur's gaze up the cliffs above them, and nodded. "I think I may follow you, Sir Arthur. I believe your solution will show us all that our God is indeed the Great Provider."

They gathered the climbing gear and as much as they could carry of their supplies in one trip, and followed Sir Arthur up the crag of rock where the tall tree stood overlooking the plateau from across the gorge.

Professor Summerlee, driven into an ill mood by the difficult climb, groaned to Sir Arthur, "Now would you be so good as to share this glorious idea with the rest of us — now that we've risked our necks climbing this cliff?"

Sir Arthur stood up, grinning proudly, and leaned against the tall tree. "Why of course, dear Summerlee. Do you notice anything unusual about this tree?"

Professor Summerlee shook his head. "Nothing in particular. Just a beech tree. I'd say, about 60 feet in height. Why?"

Sir Arthur turned to Edward. "And how far, Mr. Malone, do your sharp, young eyes perceive this gorge to be from our goal?"

"I'd say no more than 40 feet," replied Malone. "Surely you don't propose . . ."

"By george, Sir Arthur! A bridge!" exclaimed Lord Roxton. "That's usin' the old noggin!"

Lord Roxton took out an axe from their supplies and set to work at the trunk of the tree. It was a large tree, so it was quite some time before the trunk began to creak, and the tree fell across the gorge, forming a perfect bridge for them to cross over onto the mysterious plateau.

"Lord Roxton, if you don't mind, I would relish the honor of being the first to cross with you," said Sir Arthur.

"My dear chap, I really cannot allow it," replied Lord Roxton.

Sir Arthur's lip quivered. "Cannot allow it? Have I done something to offend you, sir?"

Lord Roxton chuckled heartily. "No, no, perish the thought, Sir Arthur! You're the medical man, here, and in that department, I have every confidence in you. It's just that we each have our departments, and soldierin' is mine. In a manner of speakin', we are invadin' this new country, of sorts. To barge blindly in without a bit of common sense isn't my idea of management."

Sir Arthur sighed heavily, disappointed. "And what then, would be your idea of management?"

"For all we know, sir, a tribe of cannibals could be awaitin' us on the other side of that gorge. It's better to gain wisdom *before* you land in a cookin' pot. So for now, we'd be wise to go across *hopin'* there's no trouble waitin' on us; but at the same time, we'll act as though there *were*."

"Lord Roxton, you are a wise man," Sir Arthur admitted with a nod. "After you."

Lord Roxton and Sir Arthur crossed, each carrying as many supplies as they could without endangering themselves at the dizzying height, and Sir Arthur leaped onto the rocky ground. "At last!" he exclaimed. "At last, at long last!"

Suddenly, a huge bird, taller than an ostrich, emerged from the bushes and charged toward Sir Arthur.

Before the menacing predator could reach him, however, Lord Roxton aimed his rifle, and the creature fell at the writer's feet.

As Edward and Professor Summerlee joined Sir Arthur and Lord Roxton on the plateau, they all beheld the fallen bird with wonder. Its head was shaped like that of an oversized eagle, and the cruel curve of the beak only seemed to be accentuated by the massive size. Its wings were ridiculously small in comparison to the rest of its body, and covered with mottled, bluish feathers. Its legs, though similar to those of an ostrich, were thicker and more powerful. Its talons were long, black, and shiny.

"Upon my word, Sir Arthur!" cried Professor Summerlee. "A living phorusrhacos!"

"Up until recently living, to be precise," interrupted Lord Roxton.

"But don't you gentlemen see?" Professor Summerlee explained, "A phorusrhacos is a creature from the Miocene era — millions of years AFTER the pterosaur we've seen supposedly died out in the late Cretaceous. Do you realize what this means?"

"Let's say that I do," replied Sir Arthur. "As best as I can tell, this entire plateau is the result of a tremendous geologic upheaval. The curious angle of the cliffs are seemingly immune to erosion. The jungle and all its living inhabitants — or their descendants, at least, have been spared from extinction in the world's greatest wildlife preserve."

"It also means," added Lord Roxton, "that the fossil record is at best incomplete — not to mention misinterpreted — and that all the creatures we're about to witness not only all existed at the same time, but they have existed since the beginning of creation. Creation by God, who created them — as is — and as they were. No room for improvement by any theories of 'evolution.' "

Professor Summerlee scratched his head uneasily. "Be patient with me, gentlemen, for I'm having great trouble believing everything I've ever learned in books about dinosaurs has been so misinformed. I suppose we're going to be able to revise quite a few theories in those textbooks."

"And we're going to make some publishers of dinosaur books very angry, when they realize all their text is worthless," Sir Arthur said with a chuckle. "We'll make quite a few enemies in the scientific world, as well, before this adventure is over, eh, Summerlee?"

Before Professor Summerlee could reply, there was a terrible crash behind them, and they turned to see what had happened. The bridge had given way, and sailed down into the gorge below them.

Edward cried, "What could have possibly caused that?"

"Lord Roxton!" shouted Gomez. "Lord George Roxton!" Their porter was standing beside the tree stump across the gorge, laughing wildly.

Lord Roxton stepped forward carefully. "Well, here I am," he said.

"Yes, there you are, and there you will stay!" shouted Gomez. "I nearly killed you with the stone at the cave, but this is better!"

Lord Roxton was confused. "What's this got to do with me?"

"As you lie dying up there, think of Pedro Lopez, you shot five years ago, on the Putomayo River. I am his brother!"

"I thought you looked familiar," Lord Roxton admitted angrily. "Fool that I am."

"Yes, I make fools of all of you!" Gomez shouted, dancing happily upon the tree stump. "And now that my brother has been avenged, whatever may happen now . . . I die a happy man!" As he said that, he lost his balance on the tree stump, and fell into the gorge below.

They all stood sadly. Though their betrayer would trouble them no more, they were still trapped!

Chapter 6

Marooned

No matter how hard they thought, any method of escape from the plateau seemed impossible. As they stood on the ledge, Lord Roxton did his best to comfort his companions. "Gentlemen, gentlemen! All hope is not lost! Our beloved Creator cares for the tiniest sparrows, and we are worth much more than these! Look there!"

Emerging from the bushes behind the stump was Zambo, their faithful guide. "I heard the tree fall, and then the scream of Gomez," Zambo reported. "What has happened?"

"We are victims of the treachery of Gomez," Sir Arthur explained. "But he will bother us no longer. Sadly, we remain trapped here."

"What do I do now?" asked Zambo. "You tell me and I do it."

"We have supplies already across to last us a week, if we don't find water," Lord Roxton informed them. "If we do find water, and food — who knows?"

"Zambo, inform the men below of what has happened, and make sure they don't leave us until we decide what's to be done," said Sir Arthur.

"I shall tell them, Sir Arthur," Zambo promised. "Already they have threatened to leave; they say this place is cursed."

"Make them wait until tomorrow, Zambo," Edward said. "I'll

drop down a letter somehow, to be delivered back to Mr. McArdle, my editor! First thing in the morning!"

"Yes, Mr. Malone. You don't worry. I'll make them wait." And with that, Zambo began to climb back down to the camp.

"While Zambo heads back down to our old camp, my first suggestion would be that we make ourselves a new camp, and quickly. Judgin' from Maple White's sketchbook," Lord Roxton said, looking down at the monstrous bird that had earlier attacked Sir Arthur, "this little sparrow here may be the least of our fears in this Lost World."

They found a clearing nearby, surrounded partially by a towering, rocky wall, and partially by a thicket of tall, thorny bushes. Lord Roxton suggested they complete the wall of protection by moving additional thornbushes into place. "Believe me, we'll be glad to brave the relatively minor scratches that may result, as opposed to what might happen with a lesser wall of defenses," he said.

After they had finished, and covered their thorn wounds with alcohol to prevent infection, Lord Roxton suggested they take a look around in the few remaining hours before dark. He went ahead of the party, carrying his rifle by his side as they headed into the jungle of the plateau. Professor Summerlee found a stream of fresh water, to everyone's relief, for it meant they could survive that much longer before a rescue attempt could be sent for. They followed the stream, to mark their progress, and had not gone far when they heard the sounds of large animals stomping around in the trees ahead. "Upon my word, gentlemen," exclaimed Lord Roxton. "I've encountered stampedes of elephants that make less racket than that. Stay behind me, and we'll have a look, eh?"

Cautiously, they peeked through the bushes into another clearing. There were four extraordinary creatures grazing among the leaves of the trees — two adults and two young ones. The adults were taller and by

far longer than elephants, and reptilian in appearance. They walked on all fours, but would occasionally raise their spiked forefeet up to bend branches closer as they grazed.

"Iguanodons," whispered Professor Summerlee in wonder. "Living dinosaurs! What will they say in England of this?"

"My dear Summerlee," replied Lord Roxton quietly, so as not to alert the magnificent animals to their presence, "I will tell you exactly what they will say in England of this. They will say you are an infernal liar, exactly as you and others said of me."

"What if we took them photographs?" asked Summerlee.

"Only with living specimens, as we discussed, will they be convinced," said Sir Arthur.

"Malone, I suggest you write this account and send it to your paper through Zambo tomorrow," said Lord Roxton. "Mr. McArdle may print it if he so desires. He has my permission."

As they quietly watched the animals, the largest, the one they assumed to be the adult male, was bending a tree closer to its mouth as it stood munching the leaves. Unfortunately, the mighty strength of the beast seemed too much for the trunk, which tumbled down onto the grazing iguanodon. It bleated a low warning cry, seeming to feel itself under attack, and lumbered away into the jungle, its family following behind.

"We'd best be gettin' back to camp, gents," said Lord Roxton, "so Malone has time to write his account of our adventures so far, if it's to be ready for Zambo by tomorrow morning."

Their first night in the Lost World started out as a peaceful one, until suddenly a horrible roar broke the stillness of the air. It was followed by a pitiful cry that Edward, awakening suddenly, recognized as that of the iguanodon.

By the light of the campfire, Lord Roxton stood ready for any trouble with his rifle.

"What was that?" Edward said with a shudder.

"I'm not sure," replied Lord Roxton cautiously. "But whatever it was, it's coming closer."

Indeed it was, for they heard a heavy galloping sound heading straight for their camp, and to the horror of the men they saw a lumbering shadow outside their fence of thorns. It seemed to be trying to get inside.

"Hold your fire!" exclaimed Sir Arthur. "It's just the iguanodon! We're in no danger!"

With a deafening roar, a second tremendous shadow knocked down the iguanodon and began to attack the struggling animal, until it was still. With a ferocious bellow, it aimed its head upwards as it announced victory over its unfortunate victim.

"A prehistoric carnivore!" exclaimed Professor Summerlee.

At the sound of the professor's voice, the shadowy carnivore stalked toward the camp and crouched down low to the ground as it inspected their wall of thorns.

"He's going to try to jump the fence!" cried Edward.

Lord Roxton threw down his rifle and grabbed a flaming branch from the fire, just as the large creature leaped and barely cleared the fence. Lord Roxton found himself face-to-face with a towering variety of allosaurus, an acrocanthosaurus (AK-ROW-KAN-THO-SAW-RUSS), a two-legged carnivore only slightly smaller than a tyrannosaurus, but with a short, spiny sail along its back. As it prepared itself to charge and make a quick meal of Lord Roxton and his friends, the brave hunter charged first, and shoved the flaming branch into his enemy's snout. The creature let out a bellow of pain and turned, knocking over their fence as it tried to escape the pain.

As the others stood gazing in disbelief at Lord Roxton's bravery, the hunter turned and said, almost as though nothing had happened, "Well, Professor? Ol' Spiny there was a nasty fellow. What was he?"

"I am unable to say with any certainty," muttered Professor Summerlee.

"By refusing to commit yourself, you are only showing a proper

scientific reserve," said Sir Arthur. "It would be rash to think we will be able to give a name to all the creatures we are likely to encounter."

"As we have agreed, the fossil record is at best incomplete," Professor Summerlee announced. "However, if the matter were pressed, I might suggest a megalosaurus."

"Or some variety of allosaurus," offered Sir Arthur.

Lord Roxton shook his head as the two continued their conversation into the night, and kept watch over the hole in their damaged fence. Its repair would have to wait until the morning.

At sunrise, Zambo appeared across the gorge, and Edward threw across his first letter, wrapped around a rock, which Zambo took down and gave to one of their porters. Edward and the others watched as the lone native carried his important message back to civilization. It was hard to believe that somewhere in the foggy distance was that great river along which modern steamships ran, and here they were, just outside the brink of the "modern world," defending themselves from dinosaurs.

The first business of the day was to repair the damage of their rude night visitor in the thorny wall of defense, and after once more treating their scratches with alcohol, they set out to explore the jungle. Just after they passed the glade where they had earlier encountered the iguanodon family, Edward slowed down.

"Wait just a minute," muttered Edward. "Do you hear that? It sounds . . . familiar."

Lord Roxton pointed behind them. "It seems to be comin' from this way. Let's stick close to the stream, gentleman. It seems to provide a good landmark from our camp down into the plateau."

Edward and the others agreed, and they quietly marched along until they reached a line of rocks. Lord Roxton signaled for the others to stop, and he peered over the rocks, underneath a huge, dead tree. After staring in disbelief for a few moments, he motioned for the others to join him.

Staring down into the stony pit below them, they saw a rookery of pterosaurs. Most of them sat among the rocks, while others hung from overhanging ledges, like giant bats. There appeared to be hundreds of them.

"Look at how they live in a social fashion, like penguins," whispered Professor Summerlee.

"Yes," agreed Sir Arthur. "It certainly seems to explain why the bones of this flying dragon are found clustered together."

Edward shushed his companions. "Sirs, will you please keep it down? You're going to get us in danger." Edward's voice died away into a whisper. Hanging from the dead tree directly above them was the largest pterosaur they had yet seen on their journey. Its head snapped downward and its beak opened wide with a shrill cry. All the creatures in the rookery below began to shriek in reply, and the other males soared into the sky while the females huddled protectively over their nests, covering their offspring with their wings.

"Run for your lives, mates!" exclaimed Lord Roxton. "Into the woods, where they can't fly!"

As they ran for the trees, the creatures began darting and whizzing past them. Professor Summerlee was knocked down by one, and Lord Roxton quickly helped him up and aimed his gun toward the thickening cloud of winged predators.

"The brutes mean mischief," Lord Roxton said. "He gave you a good nip with that fanged beak. I hate to announce our presence, but . . ." He fired into the swarm above their heads and one of the creatures fell to the earth, shrieking. The others, startled by the sound of Lord Roxton's rifle, flew up higher and remained circling.

"I think they're defending their territory," explained Sir Arthur. "Perhaps if we just leave . . ."

"Right," agreed Lord Roxton. "Let's get out of here before they decide to get any unfriendlier."

They hurried back toward camp, and for some time the pterosaurs seemed to follow, until thoroughly convinced that the travelers meant them no harm. Finally, as Sir Arthur and his companions reached their camp, the last of the flying creatures flapped away. "Interesting creatures," said Lord Roxton. "Did you notice the roosting place of those beasts?" he asked Edward, who nodded in reply. "Some sort of volcanic pit, wouldn't you say?"

"Exactly," said Edward.

"And the soil around the water, in those pools below the rocks?"

"I saw some bluish soil; something like clay."

"A volcanic tube of blue clay," Lord Roxton chuckled.

"What's so interesting about that?" asked Edward.

"Probably nothing," said Lord Roxton. "Anyway, when you send your next letter to your editor, prepare yourself for disbelief. From within the city, adventures like we just lived seem like a strange dream. Why, in a few months, we'll hardly believe it ourselves." The hunter's voice trailed away as they entered their camp.

All their equipment had been strewn about, and their tents had been knocked down while they had been away.

Their camp had been invaded!

"What could possibly have done this?" exclaimed Edward.

"I'm not sure," said Lord Roxton, bending down to examine the ground. "The most disturbing thing seems to be . . . they left no tracks."

"The pterosaurs?" suggested Sir Arthur.

"Maybe," said Edward, "but ever since we got here, I've had this sinister feeling we were being watched."

All of a sudden, Professor Summerlee collapsed to the ground. Sir Arthur suspected the bite the Professor had gotten from the pterosaurs may have been poisonous, so he cleaned the wound and wrapped it in bandages as best he could. While he was doing this he suggested Edward climb the tree overhanging the camp, to get a better look about the plateau. Lord Roxton boosted Edward into the tree, and he began to survey the wonderful land they had discovered.

The mysterious plateau was actually a huge, shallow funnel in shape, sloping downward to a central lake. In the sandbanks of the lake Edward could see large creatures — he guessed them to be plesiosaurs — sunning themselves on the banks. In the water, he could occasionally see large backs of animals breaking the surface. He couldn't begin to guess what they were.

Edward finally decided it was time to climb down. As he climbed past a clump of leafy branches, he found himself staring into the face of a hairy, apelike creature. For a moment, Edward and the creature were too startled to move, until finally, the ape snarled at him with a mouthful of sharp teeth, then went swinging down among the branches, and landed with a thump on the ground outside the camp, scurrying away through the leaves.

"Edward!" called Lord Roxton. "Did you fall? Are you hurt?"

Sir Arthur quickly helped Edward to the ground. "I'm all right. Did you see it? That hideous creature?"

"Nothing!" exclaimed Sir Arthur. "What did you see?"

"Some sort of ape, I think," Edward explained with a shudder. "It's probably been watching us since we arrived."

"Let's just keep our eyes open for any trouble," said Lord Roxton. "There are probably more of them, whatever they are. In the meantime, let Edward finish his map."

"Good idea," said Sir Arthur. "And since young Malone took the risk of life and limb, as it were, I think he may have the rightful honor of choosing the name of certain plateau features to his liking."

"I think I'll name the lake," Malone said, as he sketched out the map, "after my intended bride. Lake Gladys."

Lord Roxton shook his head, laughing. "Boys will be boys! Lake Gladys let it be."

Chapter 7

Constitutional

That evening, Edward had trouble sleeping. After all the adventures he had been through, he had not really had the chance to prove himself a hero, and this is what he thought Gladys wanted of him. "There are heroisms all around us," he remembered her saying. He considered going for a walk down to the lake, by himself. *Why not?* he thought.

Professor Summerlee had insisted upon taking his turn standing guard over the camp that night, despite his wound from their encounter with the pterosaurs. He still sat by the dying fire, his head wagging weakly back and forth with noisy snores. He had fallen asleep!

Edward walked right by him on his way through a small gap they had left in the fence. Edward was a fast runner, so he felt he could outrun any creature he was likely to encounter. He would be careful, he thought. He would even go all the way down to the lake, and bring back a report to his companions. And, ah, how brave they would think he was for going out exploring by himself!

If he had realized how dangerous the plateau could be, he would not have dared perform such a foolish act.

As Edward felt he should be getting close to the lake, he heard a dull, continuous roar. At first, he thought it must be another tremendous creature, shrieking its victory over an unfortunate victim. But as he got

closer, he realized it was a waterfall, and the ground almost literally fell away from underneath him as it became a steep, rocky ledge down the very side of the waterfall he had heard.

Edward now gazed down upon the lake before him, spread out like a silvery sheet, reflecting the stars above. After carefully making his way down the side of the waterfall, he bent down to the lake to get a drink. As he brought his hands to his mouth, a snakelike head emerged from the water. He fell backward, and a creature rose up out of the water toward him. It was a Saltasaurus, a four-legged dinosaur, not unlike the diplodocus, but with armored studs on its back. It rose out of the water to stomp suspiciously past Edward, while two young followed their parent out of the water.

And then, before Edward could catch his breath from his encounter with the amazing saltasaurus and its young, he saw the mighty, plated stegosaurus heading down toward the lake. It hardly seemed to notice him as it bent its head down to get a drink.

Perhaps this is the very creature that Maple White drew in his sketchbook, thought Edward. *This wonderful beast can only be a creature of God's design, not some random act of evolutionary accidents.*

Just as Edward reached out to touch the wondrous animal, the noisy roar of the predatory dinosaur rumbled down the beach. He could hear loud footsteps crashing through the jungle.

Edward ducked just in time to miss the lethal spikes of the stegosaurus' tail as it turned to run. He scurried up the ledge beside the waterfall as well as he could in his rising state of panic, and saw the stream that would lead him back to his camp, and he began to run. He ran as fast as he could for as long as he could, until at last, it sounded as though the predator was far behind him. He stopped to rest for a moment in a clearing, beside a tall, hollow tree.

A low growl nearby made Edward realize that he was not safe. He

turned to see that he had interrupted the dinner of a pair of staurikosaurs, two relatively small meat-eating dinosaurs, each about seven feet long. One of them chased Edward into the tree while the other continued eating.

They thought Edward had come to steal their dinner!

Edward realized this, amazed. *Here are two meat-eating dinosaurs,* he thought, *and this branch is well within their reach, but they're more interested in their previous kill than me! As far as they are concerned, I'm nothing more than a pesky scavenger!*

At the sound of a monstrous footstep, the two staurikosaurs scampered into the woods. Malone cringed behind the leaves of his branch as the towering acrocanthosaurus appeared in the clearing. As it leaned down to snap up the staurikosaurs' kill, Edward noticed a burn scar on its snout. It was Spiny, the same creature that had attacked their camp the previous evening!

Spiny sniffed the air toward Edward's tree and stalked forward. Edward didn't wait for him to get there, for he knew the branch was well within reach of the creature's head, so he ducked into an opening in the hollow tree.

Spiny's snout could barely reach into the opening, and Edward backed away against the inside wall of the tree.

Edward saw no possible way out. He knew that he had been foolish to go out by himself, and now it looked like the price of that foolishness might very well be his own life. Although he had not talked to God for many years, this evening had opened his eyes in many ways.

He got down on his knees and prayed.

"Lord, I know I haven't talked to You for quite some time," Edward began, and Spiny's snout shoved itself further into the opening, as some of the wood crumbled away. "And You're obviously quite busy, so I'll keep this short. Lord, please forgive me for doubting You, just because my parents died. Lord, it wasn't Your fault, so please forgive me for blaming You. I hereby acknowledge and repent of my wrongful thinking. Please, I need Your help — save me, save my spirit."

Spiny's snout snapped shut just behind his back.

"And save my skin," Edward added with a gulp. "I know I'm not worthy, Lord, but Your power and Your grace is sufficient for me. Please save me, in heaven's name, I pray."

Before Edward could finish, he heard a loud crash outside, followed by Lord Roxton's cheerful voice, "Amen!"

Edward fearfully peeked outside to see what had happened. Lord Roxton stood beside the fallen Spiny, and a large log tied to a vine was swinging back and forth from a high branch. "Good to see you, young-fellah-m'lad!" exclaimed Lord Roxton. "Looks like that prayer of yours did us both some good, what? Best shot of my entire life, and I didn't have to fire a single bullet! Just whacked the big fella against his noggin in the right spot, and boom! Over he goes!"

"You don't know how relieved I am to see you!" Edward said gratefully.

"And I to see you," replied Lord Roxton. "But don't worry

about explanations just yet, we've got to get moving! Sir Arthur and the professor have been kidnapped by those vicious apes! Follow me!"

And with that, they both ran into the jungle.

About dawn, they reached another clearing, and in a rocky wall of caves stood a place Lord Roxton called Ape Town. Dozens of the apes Edward saw earlier were moving about, and had clustered around a cliff at the edge of the plateau. The apes had cornered Professor Summerlee and Sir Arthur nearest the cliff. To Edward's astonishment, four captive natives were there, also. There were three men, and a beautiful young woman.

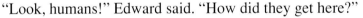

"Look, humans!" Edward said. "How did they get here?"

"I'm afraid that's not important for the moment, Malone," Lord Roxton replied. "You see that ledge? Unless we stop them, those brutes are gonna chase our professors — and all those prisoners — over the edge of that cliff!"

"How can we stop them?" asked Edward.

"I'll take care of their leader, and that ought to throw them into enough confusion for the two of us to lead them all out of there," explained Lord Roxton. "I knew it would take two of us to get those folks out of there, so I just thank the Lord nothin' happened to 'em while I went to fetch you."

Lord Roxton took careful aim with his rifle just as Professor Summerlee stumbled at the edge of the cliff, and the leader of the apes fell. Frightened by the sound, all the apes took cover in their caves. Professor Summerlee and Sir Arthur ran for the trees, and the native prisoners followed them. They all ran long and deep into the jungle, and since Lord Roxton knew the apes would try to ambush their camp, where they had first been attacked and cornered, they followed Edward's suggestion and ran to the lake. They knew they would be safer, for the time being, out in the open.

When they reached the beach of Lake Gladys, the young native woman turned to them gratefully. "You have saved us from the wild apes," she said. "We owe you our lives."

"You speak English!" sputtered Professor Summerlee. "How is this possible?"

"We were taught by Maple White," the young woman explained. "He came here to bring the message of salvation from his Savior — now our Savior as well — our Lord Jesus Christ. He also taught us many things, such as his English language. He left this place because he had been injured by the villainous creatures. Did he make it back to your world safely?"

"I regret to inform you that he did not," Lord Roxton said sadly. "But he gave us directions to find this remarkable land of yours."

"It is a great loss for our people that he is gone," said the young woman. "But he said that others would come after him to continue his work. We thank you for coming. I am Princess Maretas."

"It is a pleasure to meet you, Princess," said Lord Roxton, and he introduced the members of his party.

Lord Roxton turned to look at the lake, and was astonished to see a fleet of canoes with native warriors headed toward them. As they reached the beach, Princess Maretas waved for their attention, and she stood up on a high rock to address them.

"It is as we feared," she said. "The injury Maple White received from the apes has cost him his life, and for this, we will grieve his loss. Another tragedy I regret to announce is that before our rescue from the apes by these brave men, the apes slaughtered my father. While our ancestors may have been able to live with the apes with little incident, they have made it clear that we cannot abide their presence in our land any longer. God has sent us these brave men to assist in our battle, so that our children may grow up in a land of peace."

Princess Maretas turned to Lord Roxton, as did her people, and waited for him to speak.

"Your majesty, I believe I speak for all my friends when I say that the Lord God above brought us here for a much better reason than any of us realized. We thought we were comin' here on a sight-seein' safari, and by jove, the Lord has humbled our hearts. Your lives are in peril from these dangerous apes, and we have the means to help you. If you gentlemen are with me, Sir Arthur, I think we can only say one thing to our new friends here."

One by one, the members of their expedition nodded gravely. Lord Roxton turned back to the others, and announced, "Onward, Christian soldiers!"

The native warriors raised their spears and cheered.

"We have but to wait for the arrival of the dragons, and we will begin," said Princess Maretas.

"Dragons?" said Sir Arthur. "You mean you have tame dinosaurs?"

"We have tame dragons," the Princess corrected him. "Maple White called them dinosaurs at first, but after he saw, he referred to them as dragons."

"After he saw?" Professor Summerlee looked puzzled. "After he saw what?"

"Here they come," said Princess Maretas. "You will see, too," she said, smiling.

Galloping up the beach were tall, blue and green reptiles with curiously long crests rising back from their foreheads. Each beast was about 30 feet long, and walked on all fours, led by more natives.

"Some form of hadrosaur, or duck-billed dinosaur," commented Sir Arthur, walking toward the closest creature.

"Be careful, Sir Arthur," warned Princess Maretas. "If you get too close, he might . . ."

Just as Sir Arthur reached out to pet the animal's muzzle, it jerked its head away from him, and from its mouth it snorted flame!

The members of the party stood, their jaws hanging open in astonishment. They could not believe their eyes.

"So, they were dragons," Professor Summerlee said slowly. "They were dragons all along. Our limited vocabulary made us come up with the word 'dinosaur,' but they were dragons all along."

"My guess is that these magnificent animals have some mechanism in that stately crest," began Sir Arthur, "not unlike that of the South American bombardier beetle, which gives forth heated blasts of toxic fluid as its defense."

"I believe you're right, Sir Arthur," agreed Lord Roxton. "The curious thing that most scientists seem to forget about the bombardier beetle is that any accidental mixture of its defense chemicals would cause the creature to explode . . . if the *entire* system didn't work *just* right. If that were *not* the case, however, any incomplete version of its chemical mechanism would destroy any future descendant lines of . . . 'evolution.' An *exploded* beetle wouldn't have the chance to *reproduce* offspring with defenses that worked better than that of its deceased parent. Wouldn't you say, Professor Summerlee?"

Professor Summerlee didn't reply to Lord Roxton. He dropped down on his knees in front of all the natives, and all his fellow travelers, and bowed his head to the ground. "God, please forgive me for being a foolish, foolish man," he announced, shaking his head sadly. "I recognize You now as Creator and designer of the universe. Have mercy on me, a foolish student of science. Lord, in this one magnificent creature I have seen Your design, and I have believed. I recognize this as evidence of Your word I read . . . and rejected . . . long ago. Forgive my doubts. Amen."

"You have seen and you have believed," said Lord Roxton, as Professor Summerlee rose from the ground. "Blessed more are those who have not seen, and yet still believe."

"Amen," said Edward.

"We can discuss this later in fuller detail, gentlemen," said Lord Roxton, looking with concern into the jungle, "for here come the apes!"

Screaming and howling, the vicious apes appeared from the jungle, and charged toward the lines of the natives and Sir Arthur's friends. The twang of bows sent arrows into the midst of the angry creatures, and Lord Roxton used his rifle as a last resort to prevent any apes from getting too close. Once a creature got near enough to swing its fearsome claws at Professor Summerlee, barely missing his skull, and a shot from Lord Roxton saved the man's life. It was not long before Princess Maretas sent the dragons into the midst of the last remaining apes, and her warriors followed afterward.

"It's done," Lord Roxton said finally. "The less we see of what they do to those filthy creatures, the better we shall sleep."

Chapter 8

Accala

The next day, Edward sent across another letter to Zambo, who was greatly interested to hear about their latest adventures. Professor Summerlee remarked, after they once more discussed the issue of their escape from the Lost World, "This last adventure was enough for me, Sir Arthur. I insist that from this day forth, your primary concern is returning us once more to civilization!"

Princess Maretas showed them the place where she and her people, the Accala, lived. It was a wonderful series of small pyramids, which reminded Professor Summerlee of the ruins of ancient Mayan civilizations. In the largest pyramid there was a large room that was used as a school for the children and the other natives who wished to learn to read. Maretas and many of her people had many questions about the Bible that Maple White had left them, and Lord Roxton did his best to provide answers.

Surprisingly, Professor Summerlee turned out to be one of the most inquisitive pupils. Edward also found himself very interested, being reminded of Scripture he had forgotten since his studies many years before.

Later that evening, they were sitting among the Accala, around a campfire, eating supper.

Professor Summerlee stood up, wishing to speak. "Lord Roxton,

Princess Maretas, and all my friends, old and new," he began, "I have an announcement to make. The Scripture that we read this morning, and our discussion, led me to a very important decision on this day. I made the most important decision any man, woman, or child can make, in their entire life. I realized today that I am a sinner. I acknowledged this to our Father God, and asked the Lord Jesus Christ into my heart. Please pray for me to be faithful to Him."

Princess Maretas and her people as well as Lord Roxton and his friends applauded Professor Summerlee's decision.

"I just hope it's not too late for an old goat like me to make a positive difference in this world as a new Christian," Professor Summerlee said as he sat down beside Lord Roxton.

"It's never too late," said Lord Roxton. "One of the pleasantly curious things about Christianity is our unworthiness to be a member of His family. And you're as unworthy as they get," he added with a smile.

Professor Summerlee's wry smirk acknowledged Lord Roxton's good-natured remark, and the two shook hands.

"Sir Arthur, I thought I specifically requested you to concentrate on the matter at hand!" exclaimed Professor Summerlee. "Focus that logical mind of yours on our escape from this plateau — not on on ancient native mythology!"

Sir Arthur was bent down in the dust of one of the passages of the largest Accala pyramid, peering through cobwebs at some form of hiero-glyphics which were carved into the stone walls. Ropes had been drawn across the passage, and Sir Arthur could not resist having a quick peek, with the torch in his hand. "I'm sorry, Professor Summerlee. I just find it absolutely fascinating. Before they embraced Christianity, for hundreds, perhaps even thousands of years, the Accala seemed to believe they could communicate with the spirits of the dead. It was some form of spiritualism, similar to that which became popular in America in the mid-1800s."

Lord Roxton, Princess Maretas, and Edward walked up into the passage from another corridor. Princess Maretas looked gravely at Sir Arthur. "Sir Arthur, you need to come away from this place. We keep our shameful history recorded here only as a reminder that we should never again worship false gods."

"But my dear Princess," said Sir Arthur, "I just find all this terribly fascinating. Communicating with those who have gone on beyond this life — I would love to know more."

"No, you must not ask. After we heard the truth of Jesus Christ, we knew that our old way of life was based on a lie. And after centuries of lie upon lie, we were finally freed by truth."

"You shall know the truth, and the truth shall set you free," said Edward.

"You do realize, Sir Arthur," said Lord Roxton, taking him firmly by the arm, and pulling him under the ropes, "that if there is any spiritual contact being made, then the spirits being contacted are fallen angels."

"You mean demons?" exclaimed Edward.

"Exactly," replied Lord Roxton, leading Sir Arthur and the others back the way from which they had come. "I don't believe there are any 'ghosts of the departed' roaming the earth. That's based on the misconception I've heard that souls were either not 'bad enough' to go to hell, nor 'good enough' to make it into heaven. Either you have salvation through Jesus or you do not. Either you go to heaven or hell after death. There is no 'in-between.' "

"Sir Arthur, we beg you," said Princess Maretas laying her hand gently on his arm, "do not trouble your great mind with a wasteful pursuit that cost thousands of my ancestors their very souls."

"Do you understand what we're saying to you, Sir Arthur?" said

Lord Roxton. "This stuff is dangerous, and you need to stay away from it. All right?"

"Hmm?" Sir Arthur was glancing over his shoulder. "Oh, yes, of course. I will take everything you've told me into careful consideration. Not to worry, my friends . . . hmm . . . no . . . not to worry."

"So, Sir Arthur, as I was saying," said Professor Summerlee, "you must leave all this nonsense behind you, and return the focus of your attention to our descension from this plateau. Tell me more about this balloon idea of yours, if you would be so kind."

Professor Summerlee led Sir Arthur back up some stairs that led outside the pyramid, leaving Lord Roxton, Edward, and Princess Maretas to gaze after them with concern. "Lord Roxton, somehow, I don't think we're quite reaching him," Edward admitted, after an awkward silence.

"It would indeed be a tragedy if the creator of the ultra-logical Sherlock Holmes fell prey to a bunch of aspiring witch doctors like those spiritualists," Lord Roxton said, following a heavy sigh.

"I think he does at least know the dangers of cults," Edward replied. "He really came down hard on them *Study in Scarlet,* the first Sherlock Holmes novel. At least there's hope for the man."

"The only hope that man — or any man or woman, for that matter," Princess Maretas said, "is through Jesus Christ."

The next morning, Edward and Princess Maretas were going for a walk along the beach. They looked up to see Lord Roxton heading toward the woods in a large bell-shaped cage, which had been manufactured so that he could walk along in it. "Whatever are you doing, Lord Roxton?" exclaimed the Princess.

"Why, I'm payin' a visit to our old chums, the pterosaurs," he said. "This backward little birdcage of mine should do the job of keepin' me in and them out."

"Why would you want to go back to that horrid place?" asked Edward.

Lord Roxton seemed to hesitate. "The professor isn't the only one with, shall we say, a scientific curiosity. That's all you need to know for now."

Edward laughed in reply. "Sorry, I didn't mean to be rude in questioning your actions."

Lord Roxton returned his good-natured laugh and disappeared into the trees. "No offense taken, young-fellah-m'lad. I should see you around nightfall."

When nightfall came, Princess Maretas led Edward to a cave in the back corner of the large pyramid. "Forgive me for not showing you this sooner," Princess Maretas said. "But I was afraid that when you found you could escape this world, you would not return, and I would never see you again. You were a brave young man to come here, and bravery is something my people hold in high regard."

"What are you saying, Princess?"

"In my culture, it is the right of the female to choose a spouse, and if the choice were mine, I would choose you, Edward Malone," said Princess Maretas. "But I know you have promised to marry Gladys Hungerton."

"But that promise would do me no good if I can't return, and Princess Maretas, I have grown very fond of you," said Edward.

"Please don't make this any more difficult, Edward," said Princess Maretas. "I must tell you the truth. You can escape from this world. This is the secret tunnel through which you and your friends may return home."

Edward hugged Princess Maretas gratefully, and rushed off to tell the others.

After bidding their friends farewell, Edward and the others set out down the tunnel, and rejoined their eager companion Zambo. They gathered their supplies, and headed into the jungle that would lead them back to the canoes, and eventually, back to the mouth of the mighty Amazon River.

As soon as Sir Arthur and his friends arrived in England, there was great public uproar and curiosity, as everyone demanded to know the details of the mysterious journey. Lord Roxton had no comments for the press until the evening of another meeting of the Zoological Society.

Edward sat on the platform between Lord Roxton and Sir Arthur as Professor Summerlee addressed the members of the Royal Zoological Society. "Ladies and gentlemen, I will shortly tell you in great detail about our adventures in the hidden plateau of the Amazon, and the strange creatures we encountered there. But first, I must say that before this journey began, I made some very unkind remarks for which I now publicly apologize to my good friend, Lord George Roxton. Sir, zoology owes you and your bravery a debt of gratitude."

Lord Roxton stood and bowed to the applause of the audience, and he and Professor Summerlee shook hands. As a photographer from Edward's paper captured the historical moment on film, an angry professor rose from the platform. His name was Professor George E. Challenger, an evolutionist who had always caused trouble for Lord Roxton. He was a tall, barrel-shaped man with thick limbs, and a wild, black beard. He was every bit as irritable as his appearance suggested, and he had always been bitter toward the popularity of Lord Roxton's honorary membership in the Zoological Society.

"While I, and a number of my colleagues," argued Professor Challenger, "formerly supported Professor Summerlee's studies, I must say I am shocked. After a few months of marching around in the jungle, they come back here with these wild tales of dinosaurs and no proof!"

Lord Roxton rose quickly. "And what do you call this?" he asked, holding forth the skull of the monster bird he had shot. "This is the skull of a bird taller than any ostrich I've seen in all my years as a hunter, and it nearly cost our good friend Sir Arthur his life."

"It looks," said Professor Challenger, with a sneer, "like the skull of a phorusrhacos, and a clumsily faked one, at that."

"Are you calling me a liar?" demanded Lord Roxton. Edward and Sir Arthur had to hold him back from attacking his opponent.

"May I present to you," said Sir Arthur (after Lord Roxton had calmed down), "a small portfolio of photographs you may find very interesting."

Sir Arthur set the album on the podium before Professor Challenger, who only waved his hand in disinterest. "I saw Lord Roxton's last photograph, Sir Arthur. I was not impressed. If you recall, the object of your journey was to provide the society with a living specimen of dinosaur life."

Lord Roxton sighed wearily. "I was afraid of this. You would require to see a living specimen?"

Professor Challenger nodded. "I will accept nothing less."

"So if we had, for the sake of argument, collected a specimen for your examination, you would believe all the details of our journey?" asked Lord Roxton.

"Right down to your fire-breathing dragon," said Professor Challenger with a chuckle.

"I knew we should've left that detail out of our story," moaned Sir Arthur. "You can bet I'll leave that part out of the novel. What was I thinking?"

Lord Roxton pretended to wipe sweat from his brow. "You say we were supposed to gather a living specimen for this journey, and you will accept our tales, the bones, and photographs as factual proof, only when you behold this living specimen."

"Undoubtedly," said Professor Challenger.

"Right," said Lord Roxton. He gave a shrill whistle, and the doors at the back of the room opened. Zambo and another man entered, bearing on their backs, a large packing case. The audience, as well as Professor Challenger, let out a gasp of dismay, and silence fell over the room.

Zambo and his companion reached the platform, and looked to Lord Roxton, who nodded. Zambo took out a key and unlocked the padlock.

"Ladies and gentlemen, the honor of our word has been questioned," said Lord Roxton. "I now invite Professor Challenger to live up to his word, and examine, to the best of his ability, the living specimen which we now present as evidence to the Royal Zoological Society of our wondrous journey."

Professor Challenger stepped up to the case as Lord Roxton opened the lid. "They probably stuck some elephant's tusks on some poor pussycat to convince me they found a saber-toothed tiger cub," said Professor Challenger with a sneer as he stepped forth.

"Come then, pretty, pretty," said Lord Roxton, and Professor Challenger leaned forward.

With a scratching, rattling sound, a pterosaur hopped up on the edge of the box and hissed in the face of Professor Challenger, who fell backwards off the platform. Two ladies screamed, and several members of the audience began to make for the door.

"Ladies and gentlemen, please

control yourselves!" pleaded Lord Roxton, throwing up his arms. The sudden movement frightened the pterosaur, and it unfurled its wings, and began to circle the room, which only startled the crowd that much worse.

"The window!" exclaimed Sir Arthur. "For pity's sake, close that window!"

It was too late. Seeing an escape route, the creature flapped out the window, and following its homing instinct, flew over the rooftops of London, and toward the sea. A report came later from a ship called the SS *Friesland* that the crew had sighted a creature which appeared to be a cross between a "flying goat" and a "monstrous bat" heading southwest.

After the cheers for the heroes at the meeting and a public apology from the suddenly humble Professor Challenger, Lord Roxton invited his friends over to his apartment for a private celebration. "I'll be over shortly," Edward promised him. "First I have to go see Gladys. I had hoped she would be here, but I didn't see her."

"We'll toast your marriage when you return," said Lord Roxton. "Hurry along, now!"

———   ———   ———   ———

Edward stood upon Gladys' front porch, wondering what to do. He knew now that he was indeed a Christian, and as a Christian, he could not possibly marry Gladys — she was not a Christian. He could only go in and try to explain that to her as best as he could.

Edward dashed into the same living room that started his adventure, where he saw Gladys sitting quietly. She looked up in surprise as he exclaimed to her, "Gladys, my dear little Gladys Hungerton!"

"Whatever do you mean?" she asked.

"Aren't you my dear Gladys . . ." Edward began.

"My name is now Gladys Potts," she corrected him. "Let me introduce you to my husband."

Edward shook hands with a gentleman that he had not seen sitting in the room behind him.

"It's a pity — you must have not gotten my letter," Gladys said. "It would have made everything clear."

Edward smiled. "Oh, it's all quite clear." He turned to Gladys' husband. "So, Gladys wanted to marry an adventurer, and she married you. So what did you do? Find a hidden treasure? Discover a lost continent? Do time on a pirate ship?"

"Er, I'm a," stuttered the man with some difficulty. "I'm a solicitor's clerk."

"Ah," said Edward. "Good night," he said, and closed the door behind him as he vanished into the evening.

Edward stopped on the street and looked up toward the starry sky. "Heavenly Father, sometimes Your sense of timing amazes me. Thank You, Lord."

And with that, he headed over to Lord Roxton's.

———   ———   ———   ———

"Quite sorry to hear about your canceled engagement, young-fellah-m'lad," said Lord Roxton after Edward explained to his friends his experience at Gladys' home. "But it simply wasn't God's will, and I think we can all content ourselves with that. Anyhow, I've got some good news that should take your mind off it for the time being, at least." He brought out an old cigar box from a cupboard and placed it on the table before Edward, Sir Arthur, Professor Summerlee, and Zambo.

"Anything will be welcome," said Edward.

"I possibly should have said something about this before, but I didn't want to get anyone's hopes up without reason," Lord Roxton said, scratching his head. "But then it was fancy, and now it's a fact."

"Lord Roxton, whatever are you talking about?" Professor Summerlee inquired excitedly.

"Edward may well remember I commented that the pterosaur rookery was a volcanic vent of blue clay," Lord Roxton continued as Edward nodded. "And in all my travels, I've only known one other volcanic vent with blue clay. That would be the great De Beers Diamond Mine of Kimberley, right? So I get diamonds into my head, I make myself a little protective, portable bird-cage, and here's what I find."

Lord Roxton spilled the contents of the box onto the table. There were 20 rough stones or more, varying in size from that of beans to the size of chestnuts. "On my first day back I took them over to Spink's and had them roughly cut and valued. These may not look like much at first, but here's the result of that trip."

Lord Roxton opened a pillbox from his shirt-pocket to display one of the most beautiful, glittering diamonds Edward had ever seen. "I was told the lot runs a rough minimum of two hundred thousand pounds. The adventure would not have been possible minus any given man at this table, so I insist on fair shares between all of us. Well, Sir Arthur, what shall you do with your forty thousand?"

"If you persist in your generous proposal," said Sir Arthur, "I should, with my wife, take a holiday among a primitive people. The Accala of South America, I should think."

"Princess Maretas' people?" said Lord Roxton. "I was thinking of payin' those folks an extended missionary visit myself, with my share. Professor Summerlee, what about you?"

"I must say, my dream has often been to found a private museum, but your plans seem far more admirable," replied the elderly Professor.

"Why not dedicate your museum to creation science?" suggested Lord Roxton.

"Creation science," muttered Professor Summerlee. "A dinosaur museum dedicated to creation science. Yes, I rather like that term. Zambo, what shall you do? That's a lot of money, you know."

"The money matters little to me," replied Zambo. "I should like to have a closer look at this Lost World for myself. I frankly felt left out of your last journey. I will return with Lord Roxton, and of course, Sir Arthur."

"This adventure, like all the best ones, seems to have written itself," replied Sir Arthur. "I imagine I shall have to change very little before it gets to print."

"Will we all be there?" asked Professor Summerlee. "As I mentioned earlier, I should very much like an autographed copy."

"Of course, dear Summerlee," replied Sir Arthur. "You will be there, brave young Malone will be there, the mighty hunter Lord Roxton will be there, as will the faithful Zambo. I don't really care to include myself as a character, so I think I'll replace my position in the tale with that of grumpy old Professor Challenger. His 'powder-keg personality' will be a refreshing change from that stuffy Sherlock Holmes.

"Hopefully, my editor won't change too much. It's distressing, sometimes, the changes they suggest. But at least Lord Roxton's generous gift will enable it to see print, one way or another."

"And Malone, what of you?" asked Lord Roxton with a grin. "What will you do with all of your share?"

"If you will have me," Edward said. "I would very much like to join the rest of you in having a better look at the dear old plateau."

Lord Roxton extended his hand to Edward. "We wouldn't go without you. And if you don't mind me sayin', I think someone there will be very happy to see your return. A certain native Princess, perhaps?"

At this the men laughed, and Edward could only blush in reply.

THE END

AUGUST 10, 1897

Natives refer to this beast
as 'the Great Stalker'

Flying
Scavengers

Male Stegosaurus
and Friend

Various sketches & Watercolor Studies
from Maple White's Diary/Journal

Afterword

It is truly puzzling that for all the sophistication of the wondrous sculptures and monuments produced by the ancient Egyptians (not to mention their architectural achievements that still impress us today) that they worshiped frogs and dung beetles. And, as intellectual as we often give them credit for being, it is said they thought the brain was simply an oversized organ that produced mucous.

It is just as equally puzzling to me that the creator of Sherlock Holmes, quite possibly the greatest advocate for logic and reason in Western literature (and author of some of my own favorite English literature — notably the original 1912 novel *The Lost World*, despite its annoying references to evolution), should become an advocate for spiritualism.

Sadly enough, toward the end of Sir Arthur Conan Doyle's life he became so obsessed with spiritualism that he lectured on it, and eventually wrote a book on it. His real-life friend, Harry Houdini (who made a career of exposing frauds such as mediums), was very skeptical of Doyle's adopted "religion," and rightfully so.

Any religion, if it is not based on the saving grace of Jesus Christ, the Son of God, who offered himself as a living sacrifice for the sins of all mankind (as revealed in the Bible), is a false one, and all the labor of those who practice that religion is in vain. You can't work your way into heaven, so don't exhaust yourself by trying. All you can do is accept God's gift of grace.

We are saved by grace, and not by works (Eph. 2:8–10).

We are sinners by nature, yet saints by God's grace.

I pray that if you do not already embrace Jesus Christ as your Lord and Savior, that you will do so. Please pray about it. And please, if you feel led to do so, pray with your church's pastor or youth minister in more depth. I'm sure they would be happy to hear about your concern regarding where you will spend eternity.

For further information on how you can know the Lord Jesus Christ, contact Answers in Genesis at P.O. Box 6330, Florence, KY 41022-6330, and ask for a free booklet about the free gift of salvation.

About the
Author-Illustrator

Mark Stephen Smith got his degree in graphic design from Auburn University Montgomery, where he occasionally teaches video animation. He has written six novels, 30 short stories, and a few more short stories in comic book format. This, however, is the first of his works anyone has dared to publish. His interests (besides Christianity and dinosaurs, which should be obvious) are animation,cryptozoology, puppetry, science fiction films, British humor, and making people doubt his sanity by doing really goofy voices.

Like most creative people, Mark has performed quite a few jobs, including math tutor, radio announcer, movie doorman and concession stand worker, T-shirt designer, and most recently, multimedia specialist.

He hopes to see *The Lost World Adventures* produced as the first Christian theatrical animated feature (and he longs to provide several of the voices, notably the goofy ones).